Falling Through the Music

MARK HALPERIN

Falling Through the MUSIC

Univeristy of Notre Dame Press
Notre Dame, Indiana

Library of Congress Cataloging-in-Publication Data

Halperin, Mark.
Falling through the music / Mark Halperin.
p.   cm.
ISBN-13: 978-0-268-03081-0 (pbk. : alk. paper)
ISBN-10: 0-268-03081-2 (pbk. : alk. paper)
I. Title.
PS3558.A396F35   2007
811'.6—dc22

                              2006039803

for

B

CONTENTS

III

IV

ACKNOWLEDGMENTS

Some of these poems, at times with other titles and/or in other versions, have appeared in the following publications:

88: A Journal of Contemporary American Poetry, "On Certainty" and "Parakeet"

Denver Quarterly, "Buying Jewelry in St. Petersburg" and "Growing Up"

Iowa Review, "Blue Heron" and "The Trouble with Spring"

m.a.g. (on-line journal), "Other Rooms"

Natural Bridge, "Rembrandt's *Prodigal Son*"

NeoVictorian/Cochlea, "Among the Dead"

Notre Dame Review, "Notes on the Russian Elevator," "Now and Then" and "Saint Petersburg to Moscow Train"

Pacific Review, "My Mother's Words"

Paper Street, "Waking to Love"

Paumanok Review, "Other Languages" and "Returns"

Poems & Plays, "Retirement"

Pontoon #4, "Fear"

Prairie Schooner, "Accident," "Lines," "Lying," "Orders," "Pop," "Sincerity," and "Talonachkaya Vodka"

Quarterly West, "On a Theme from Donne," "Padua," and "Strokes"

River Styx, "Tulips" and "Babel"

The Saint Ann's Review, "Autumn Elsewhere"

Seneca Review, "Valentine"

Sentence, "At the Concert"

Sycamore Review, "Reading at the Beach"

Smartish Pace, "Someone Pausing"

Timber Creek Review, "Guildenstern to Horatio"

"Tulips" was reprinted in *Poetry Daily*, the website and the book, Diane Boller, Don Selby, and Chryss Yost, editors, Sourcebooks, Inc. Naperville, Ill, 2003.

Most of section II appeared in *NEAR AND FAR*, a chapbook published by March Street Press, Greensboro, North Carolina.

I thank Michael Collier, Jonathan Jonhson, Steve Orlen, Joseph Powell, Terese Svaboda and Richard Terrell for their assistance with the contents and shape of the manuscript.

I

READING AT THE BEACH

I believe Celan because he jumped into the Seine and drowned,
and Dickinson because she didn't marry,
and Mandelstam because he tried to write a poem for Stalin that would
    save his wife and maybe himself, and did write one, though he per-
    ished all the same.

And I believe Stevens because he continued to live in a large brick house
    with a wife who didn't love him or he didn't love, and went to the
    office everyday;
and I believe Bishop because when the money ran out, she found work,
and Baudelaire for keeping to one book, like Whitman, at about the same
    time too.

I believe Rilke because looking, for him, was looking into, and so I
    overlook his fascination with titled women,
and believe Yeats for making the aristocratic seem noble,
and Tsvetaeva for coming back to rage at everyone, even while the Terror
    was raging around her, even if she hanged herself with the piece of
    rope Pasternak reputedly gave her to tie her bags,
and Williams for living in Paterson, New Jersey of all places, dancing like
    an uncle, while doing some serious fooling around,
and Auden for being generous after he was disappointed in love, and for
    drinking martinis in England, which was very American.

Without the verification of their lives, how could I trust them?
So what if Donne, born a Catholic, ended up the head of the Anglican
    Church?
So what if Baratinski, who died shortly after his beloved wife, worshiped
    Goethe?

And I withhold judgment on the living, as I read toward twilight;
I don't ask how long will I turn back to this one or that one.

The roar of the sea drowns out questions,
it goes on and on where I am;
the sun hangs above the water, laying down a path like a set of stepping-
    stones that shimmer even as they grow small, shrinking to a single
    point of light.

POP

He had been Austrian, he told me, and when I was young, I imagined him in Vienna, its waltzes and tankards of foaming beer. The few times I was taken to his apartment, confined to the kitchen, I would peer at the living room, always dim in late afternoon sunlight, and study the furniture, the hulking sofa and easy chairs covered in thick, cloudy vinyl, the room no one used.

Sunday mornings, when he ate with us, there were bagels, butter or cream cheese, and whitefish, lox, sardines, big cups of coffee with milk and sugar. Finished, well-chewed cigar between his teeth, he'd climb into a DeSoto or Dodge the rich maroon of gravy, one stop completed on the rounds of his three children, and disappear.

His actual birthplace, I learned, was on the frontier of the Austro-Hungarian Empire, Czernowitz—city of Paul Celan, who wrote in German, Rumanian, translated Mandelstam, who, family murdered by the Nazis, fled to Bucharest, and finally, in 1970, the Seine.

After Pop, as my mother called him, died, I studied the remote corners of Europe for a city that kept moving: to Rumania, Moldavia, Ukraine, the Soviet Union. I scanned maps for mysterious Bessarabia, which I adorned with palm trees, then the adjacent Bukovina, of which it was the capital, until I'd pinned it down: Czernowitz, city on the River Bug, Cernauti, city with the changing name, Chernivts of five languages, Cernauti cleansed by Nazis, Soviets, Rumanians, Cernivtsi, like Pop, irrecoverable.

When Mother called to say
father was dying, I didn't ask
for time to make arrangements.
My wife said she'd inform
my boss. I packed, drove to
the airport and flew cross-
country, feeling proud I'd
thought of him and her before
myself, although I'd paused
on the phone and mother must
have heard. When, years later,
my sister called and said, *Sit down*
I knew before a word, Mother
had died. This time I left with-
out false self-congratulations,
wanting Mother to be proud,
to hear her say "You did well"
who'd sent me back then, before
my father died. *You've a wife,*
a child, another life: go home.

GROWING UP

1.

I believed my father was a spy. He had been born in Russia, he had an accent, and he was older than other dads, which confirmed it. He was always disappearing into the basement—to work, he said. I guessed he sent secret messages to Moscow late at night. If they caught him, I would defend him, but I knew what he was doing was wrong. I loved him *though* he was a spy.

In the Soviet Union, I had learned at school, people had no liberty, but he argued education was free there: college, even medical-school. Later, when I asserted the superiority of the Soviet Union's treatment of women, he angrily informed me that women doctors were paid less than men who dug ditches. He kept me unbalanced, uncertain. No matter which side I took, he took the other. No matter what I believed, what I believed was wrong and based on insufficient knowledge. Father knew if you knew more . . .

2.

My father wasn't a spy, though he did spend a lot of time in the basement, where he worked on plaster casts, the furnace, and making cabinets. He could have been thinking. Maybe English didn't feel comfortable or we didn't in those days, in his late forties. Then I was almost grown and he was old. He stayed upstairs, even more a mystery. Polite, handsome in an Old World way, with generous, deep, sad eyes, he could be mercilessly ironic with me.

3.

Since Father was never a regular dad, that role devolved to Mother, a native-born American and accentless. I fought with her rather than my father. She liked the brio of engagement, the stir of conflict, but our disputing horrified him, who was the youngest, last and twelfth, or the twelfth of thirteen. He had been raised by sisters he loved absolutely. How could a child argue with his mother?

I lost regularly and the battles were drawn out, but I'd find a wedge of Swiss-cheese in the refrigerator, a peace offering.

4.

After my father died, I thought of everything I didn't know about him and never would. I still do. His distance remained as if it were all that could be saved. One day, after my mother died, I came across my camera. What did I need it for? Who would I send pictures to?

LYING

Why you might feel uncomfortable
    with elaborate weavings, when
they're as apt to catch on hard fact
    as to unravel or become one
more maze you'd forgotten the way out
    of, any one could understand.
The prudent shun a purely gratuitous

    complexity. But this reluctance
to pretend you enjoyed a meal, a book—
    to say to someone you may not
like, *nice to see you*, when it's to your advantage
    to do so, this pulling back as from
a foul smell or window ledge. . . . Why
    fudge, why resort to a "modified

version," mislead, concoct, invent, rather
    than simply lie? Do we intuitively
regard the false, not as unreal, but unclean?
    Are the keenly ironic, ambiguous
phrases we toss off—our evasions and/or
    shufflings, those clever side-steps
we do in dancing—done to hide the truth, to

    keep it from harm's way, secure it
a place for safekeeping? From whom or what?
    Or is it us? Discretely bending
the data, smearing a line you'd just as soon
    not cross, you're not a fraud
so much as someone hedging his bets, testing
    the ground, noting a nearest window,

door in case an unexpected exit's called for.
    When was it that simplicity sufficed
and like a captured soldier all you had to give
    was a name, rank, and serial number,
and gentlemen—their sacred word? Before
    the invention of torture, was honor
worth more? Was it all there was to lose?

SINCERITY

There are those who shake
at the thought of being obscure,
ingenuous, and turn to memory
as a wall they can lean against,
rock solid, its guarantees basic
as desire's gutturals. The facts
and their significance they trust

blindly. Still, I recall the taste of
my own stomach's churning, hot
breath in my face. Squeamishness
felt then fled, and I reached down
deeper than I ever had before for
any scraps to feed the laboring
engine of my ingenuity. Say

"Freedom is the recognition
of necessity," as Benedict Spinoza
did, who never taught, but bought
his own with a shorter life by
grinding glass. Sincerity may
just be the overrated ballast,
to jettison when you need speed.

GUILDENSTERN TO HORATIO

Nothing fit but you, as tranquil as
a lake, and your biography, like glass,

transparent. You were always handy, tame,
forgettable, without a second name—

and for the aristocracy, friend
and servant are so close they seem to blend.

You might have penned a more reliable
version of events, played down your role until

the epilogue, bloody but tidy. Who
else could the young Fortinbras turn to?

OTHER LANGUAGES

If body language, the way
breathing speeds up, levels
off and slows, the involuntary
shudders that take and shake
us head to foot, encourage
understanding, then we still
need our tongues for more
than French kisses. When

they convey endearments,
do the hushes of Russian
foster whispering, the level
stress of Japanese, an elegant
minimalism? If even low
currents of voices, hurried
mumbles among fumblings,
have the potential to shock

and burn, what can protect
us? Maybe those barriers—
cultural as much as linguistic,
cordoning off a licensed 'this'
from a forbidden 'that'—fall,
and in speech that passes language,
we comprehend the other
stripped still more naked. Is

audio-dress, when there is
little else, just enough to cover
pleasure? It could be each time
we come together, my dear,
for all we've learned of how
or who or where we are, we are
 undone, and must start again
from scratch to learn the language.

RETIREMENT

Speech, they're shouting to those who will retire,
whose desks and lockers will be cleaned out, who'll leave
offices and parking spaces like prizes
for others to fight over. They're prompting: *a few*
words for the microphone—shared memories
like searchlights in front of a new business

to draw in the onlookers. It's a curious business,
these send-offs at which the colleagues of those who retire
assemble and linger over their collective memories.
Remember when you shaved off your mustache? Can you believe
we couldn't tell what was wrong: a few
thought you were sick, others, stuck up,—surprised

when you explained. Or was the real surprise
their barely visible smirks? It's nobody's business
where the implications went, how few
they were, and how they've blurred. You tire
of distinguishing what happened, from what you believe
might have, invention from memory.

Fine as scars or wrinkles, memories
mesh, crosshatch, fuse. As one pries
free another falters. It's a relief
when someone fills in the details, sorts out the business
of who said what to whom, who was drunk or tired,
sentimental or snide. Among the few

remainders are the limits, the borders and curfews
that tell you to turn back, memories
are places to get lost in. Soon, too tired,
too toothless for experience, you prize
traces of fine workmanship, your business,
appreciation of the past. It's a relief

when things work, aren't dangerous, a relief
when burdens can be left behind like a few
illusions or extra pounds, the funny business
of sex. Simplify—memories
are accidents, you say, helpers. Apprised
they're not needed, they gracefully retire

as, when you leave, you hope to, tired
of the present's busyness: the past, a few
memories, the future, blank surprise.

In the mist of sleep, I think: dogs—
so many in the street they're nipping,
running and snapping at each other—
tiny noises, pitch rising
in frequency, and persistent—till
even asleep I know the cries
come from my unknown, unseen
neighbors on the other side
of one thin wall. A pause, and I wake
more alone than before as they
start up again, gasp to gasp,
one, not quite there. Yesterday,
at the Polyclinic, I trailed a nurse
from the consulting room. As we turned
a corner women students were pulling
their blouses on. Unconcerned,
she waved me through. There was, is,
nothing to avoid—no door to shut
and nowhere to go. Don't ask me
obvious questions. I made my way
back then as I do now, in this narrow
bed, imagining your sweet body.

REMBRANDT'S *PRODIGAL SON*

I.

The boy's back, thick and richly clad though poorly
        formed, hunkers, a stone the father faces,
blindly facing out. And the others, holding back, what
        could they say?—that we are no more than
uneven surfaces the light plays on, revisited at angles
        it commands, graced and humbled equally:
father, his returned son, figures and ground, viewer
        and guard? I recall the father's tipping
forward, the boy's crouch, fanning rivulets of paint.

2.

The standing figure, joined hands, head cast back
and the first of the figures in shadow, further back,
and back still further, higher, a dim face floating
like a prisoner. There. There. The son, in tatters,
the mask of his face on his father's breast, shape
clear, features lost in the first of many shadows.

Upper left—something's looming. Today's
clouds and the glare and sheen of oil hide it
as the father's wealth almost obscures his
blindness, the dollops of white paint laced with
black suggesting pearls he cannot see as we
cannot see the tall windows that illuminate
this stage of their meeting or into the shadows

advancing to envelop young and old, bearded,
clean-shaven, and the smooth-faced. White
dribbled onto a rough edge catches like froth
to claim the eye a second. There. An image buried
in the upper left-hand darkness resolves a moment—
a face in this world—or have we entered shadows?

3.

Here the colors time favors, velvety
blacks, reds, browns, and ochres
bleed and fade into the background

which has almost absorbed one figure—
in the upper right—as the father's
embrace has almost taken in his son's face.

Think of music—not sound, but
rendered emotion: how the simple
grows complex as if evading ear

and understanding, to lodge at last
in memory where all layers meld.
And now the lights flash off and on.

You could be turning your eyes
from an intimacy you find embarrassing
to witness or leaving for one of your own.

BABEL

It seemed another morning. Each man rose,
yawned, stretched and maybe washed, pulled on his clothes,

grabbed bread and headed off for work. Each thought
of how they climbed, how months of labor brought

the end a little closer. What they'd do
once they reached the sky, the shell of blue

breached, and they passed, as through an open gate—
to Heaven!—they had no time to contemplate.

They started for work earlier each day.
One noon no different from the others, they

were different. It was nothing you could touch
or see. The air trembled. With not so much

as a leaf flutter, birds were circling. Someone
paused and asked for more mortar, come

to the end of this row or that. Nothing came.
He turned to find out why and met the same

confusion on every side. It multiplied
through a hundred thousand others, wide-eyed,

each of them stunned silent, as when you wake
somewhere you don't remember, the disk of a lake

shining in the distance. They recognized
the faces, shifted or skewed, but otherwise

familiar, like synonyms. Their words had changed
but their meanings were unaltered. How strange

to be transported to this world, a hell,
where no one was at home and none could tell—

stripped of a common language to express
it in—what that felt like. They stood defenseless,

as men had never been and never would
again. That was all they understood,

and all understood it perfectly that one
last time before they left—their tools, the tower—done.

II

RETURNS

A friend asks why I keep returning to Russia, and I talk about people in a "march-route" taxi passing fare-money to a passenger in the front. She hands it over to the driver, who makes change, then the process reverses, money passing down the line. I like the odd community. I say, it's become a place I can enter, full of connecting alleys and friends. Don't I know which central market has the lowest prices, and to ask who's last, when I join a line? Where else could I use that? Those I love and have loved are people I was irresistibly drawn to, pursued, and at the same time, those who let me pursue them—one place, one time. Isn't that a life, mine, and like a poem, shouldn't it appear inevitable and freely elected, the contradiction joined in who I am? Suppose that woman had had blue eyes or I had lost this man's address or no one answered the phone.

AFTER THE CRASH,

when I slid out the unbashed-in side
of the car, I didn't think of just how close I'd
come to dying or my good luck:
I reassured the two cops I was fine,
then the kids who hit me and maybe myself. I signed
something for the driver of the wrecking truck.
He pulled away, and I called my wife, brushed glass
from my hair, then sat down on the curb to pass

the time until she came for me, waiting
for it to sink in. There was the sting
of antiseptic at the hospital,
focus and knee-reflex tests, a slowed
down pulse and in my scalp a gash they closed
with four, bright, stainless steel staples.
Later, my ribs would ache; it would be hard to breathe
and I'd walk with an invalid's care, but I didn't believe

I was changed. Only today, a year and a half
later, when someone asks about it, I laugh
then feel the collision that I never felt
before I blacked-out—an acknowledgment
of fear I didn't think to make then, content
I hadn't lost a trip abroad. It's the guilt
without reason of survivors who react
much later, the slide and blank after impact.

BUYING JEWELRY IN SAINT PETERSBURG

Across the street from the museum, which was once a palace, a middle-aged woman wearing a crimson housedress, a shawl and slippers opens the door. She gathers up her lap dog to let us pass below the boar's head into the apartment. Here ceilings rise fifteen or twenty feet on wallpaper darkened by cooking. We've come for gemstones of a quality "that does not exist in the stores," she says, sold at prices "two or three times lower than in the stores"—which, if it doesn't quite make sense, suggests good luck.

But first there are paintings to look at, a marble fireplace, and we must hear the apartment's story, which is her family's before the revolution and after. You can tell this is a preface she has told many times, like the information about which stones protect against lost love and the draining moon. She says they were "repressed," a verb compassionately vague, suggesting train rides, taiga and birches without end, rather than "the end" the camps were, the years excised from lives that only sometimes started up again. *Rasstrelyat*, to execute by firing squad, is specific as a splash of chilly local color.

The lamps come on and I'm lost with the others. She spills out bags of amethysts, the pure pigments of garnets, trays with the coiling sheen of freshwater pearls. The moonstones seem to hover and there is jasper, lapis—agate in necklaces and pins and rings. Time grows confused. Our conversations lag. The hours run together like stiff smiles. Then it's time to say good-bye and pay. Tired of strangers petting him, the dog pulls back his lips on teeth like yellowed ivory and growls.

NOTES ON THE RUSSIAN ELEVATOR

1.

The Russian elevator has no memory. Before two people on the ground floor enter the cab, each announces a floor. The one whose floor is higher enters first, followed by the other, who then presses a number. God help you if more than two people are present. Breathing will be hard; the cabs are small. When the first exits, the second immediately presses a number. If there is a pause and someone on the ground floor presses the call button, the person in the elevator will have to ride down to the ground floor, at which point the process will recommence.

2.

Getting the elevator on a winter morning, when the stairs are dark because the sun rises late and light bulbs disappear or break, requires luck. If the elevator is moving when you hit the button, your call will not register. If someone hits the button on another floor after the elevator stops and before you have a chance to hit the button, your call will not register. Russians believe they are a patient people and it is possible their elevators know this. More likely, the creators of the Russian elevator knew this and designed them with it in mind.

3.

Elevator cabs are sometimes used as "rest rooms." This may be due to their small size, which makes them resemble toilet stalls. It may be due to the needs of those on the street. Whichever is the case, should you succeed in calling the elevator, scan the floor before you enter, and then immediately press your number.

4.

The cab of an elevator is often decorated with writing, declarations of love or curses or experiments in Russian or other languages. I once saw a drawing of circle below which were the Russia letters that are the equivalents of "IVA." What is "IVA"? Then I realized that just as English speakers see one Russian letter as a reversed "R," so Russian speakers see an English "N" as a reversed Russian "I." What I was looking at was intended to represent "NBA"—the circle was a basketball. Russians love basketball. The broken buttons for the floor selection and the holes in the cab are different forms of decoration. It doesn't matter what they mean.

NOW AND THEN

Wasn't the present to be that knife-edge
on which the past and future tottered,
cleanly dividing them, with no saving up
or weighing consequences, not this
effort against that result? Wasn't the past

to contain no more than old habits,
and love to be not simply prelude to grief,
source of soiled hopes that beggared,
riddled and despoiled the view? Remember
a bridge, a rise from which the square

opened in snow, the marble, angel-topped
column in the distance and a dome?
Remorse could wash you one last time
and each parting seem the final one,
unique in its own diminished future.

OTHER ROOMS

The Bonnard triptych was hanging in the former Czarist General Staff Headquarters Building in St. Petersburg, just across from the Winter Palace. We had just come down three flights of stairs from the painting of a park, the Mediterranean shimmering turquoise behind it, over-arching trees, children and two women, one with a blue parrot that Bonnard painted for the house of some fabulously rich Russian in Moscow. I turned to the woman who had taken our tickets saying, *Absolutely marvelous. I've never seen such a large Bonnard of such high quality*, showing off my Russian, love of art and trying to be friendly all at the same time. But she was primed for something else. *Yes, indeed, it is good, and it's good for you. In former days, when we didn't have warm clothes all the time, Russian babushkas used to dress in red. It keeps you warmer*, she said, then told me how colors were like medicine and asked if I knew about Yoga and *chakras*, which was beside the point since she was explaining the seven of them, the lower ones, more animalistic, she said, associated with sex and base energies, with the note "la," and the higher ones, blue and violet—I've forgotten with which notes. She was all full steam ahead, and another woman, sitting in the chair she had vacated, nodded—it was hard to know whether in agreement or just following the rhythm and letting the words rock her.

AT THE CONCERT

As always, I drift off. They're playing Bach. As the new spaces in his
music keep opening, I find myself recalling Jan, dead less than ten
months. Years ago, when he danced, he'd find, in falling, ways to
land no one expected, as Bach does, to our delight. I remember how
friendship outlasted his skirts, sex roles, our many differences—and
we were writing twice a week, until the cancer ate away his breath.
And then the music's back, Bach's roller coaster. I'm tapping my
foot, the man to my right not sure where to place me. Opening after
opening. I think of my mother: rather than ask me why I was here
again, a place she thought of as dangerous, she'd have tried her worry
out on a dozen friends. She died not knowing I planned to come back
again. The man to my left doesn't care for the violinist in the trio. He
shakes his head. They're playing Strauss, now, pure *schmaltz*. What's
the Russian for that? What's the English? All I can't hear gives me
trouble now, as the dead do, falling through the music.

FEAR

You hear stories: the man robbed
in the market, the woman on a bus
who looked down to find her purse
gone—fast fingers, sharp blades,
policemen who want money. You
could be struck crossing the street
if someone didn't call out in time.
Fear's the bird searching for crumbs,
none too picky, the dog looking for
doorways in the rain, a man with a knife
who'll take you on at the right moment.
It's me as object of myself, demanding,
out of patience, my fatigue giving in,
me, fought out, backing into myself.

LOVE'S NEEDS

for B

Even our bodies, much
as they happily differ, relate
one story. Let them touch
and they are complements:

push matches yield, groan trades
with sigh. We fall in stride,
hold on tight while riding.
Though the floor rocks, you're firm

enough to lean on, to turn to,
as I do, wherever I am or you
are in me, as if the years
we'd lived together grew

eloquent and calmed me, ballast
or cargo, our trade, my dear,
in one another, free of
all but love and love's needs.

How it's done comes back to me when the women—one maybe twenty-two, the other, her mother—enter the coupe. *Good evening*, the well brought-up daughter says, and I reply, *good evening*. We hang our coats and as she turns I see a single braid reaching to the top of her thighs. She's not five feet tall, sniffling—a cold, the flu or grippe. Her mother, heavyset, maybe forty-five, fifty, strokes her cheek and feeds her pills. It seems the daughter's crying. They start putting bags away under the lower bunk, which lifts—yes, that's why it's preferred: no one can reach your things. They set out slippers. A man joins us, plumpish, in his twenties. The mother offers him room under the bunk, as I should have, but he's content with the upper storage space, a sort of tunnel over the corridor. When the conductor comes for tickets, our late arrival offers his, pulls out a cigarette, uncaps a beer and leaves. We give ours, then the daughter reaches for one of the rolled, thin mattresses above, pillows, plastic bags with sheets, makes up her mother's bed and then her own. I stand in the corridor until she's done, then make up mine. The conductor's back to collect for sheets, and the young guy with him, but briefly. I remember to step outside again to let the women undress. *Please close the door*, the girl asks from the upper berth. Policemen start down the aisle, knocking on compartment doors, peering in. The young guy and I reenter. He unrolls his mattress, not bothering with the sheets, and leaves. When he comes back I'm still awake and the mother's reading light still on. I hear him snoring, see the girl reach over to shake or talk to him as she never would to me. He stops. The mother's light goes out. I sleep in spurts, feel the train's sway and stopping. I've only napped, I think, when the sharp knock comes to tell us it's 45 minutes to Moscow. Then I've pulled on pants and shirt, stand outside the coupe again as the women dress. They're having breakfast, the young guy's still asleep, as the train rolls into the station. *Have a good day*, I say to the women. The girl unbraids and rebraids her hair. Mother sweeps up crumbs with her hand. Both turn: *Safe trip*.

AUTUMN ELSEWHERE

The statues are not covered yet, nor the trees
wrapped; that will come. But heaps of leaves fill
the *allées,* a few people stroll, and swans circle
the edges of the pond, still fed. Any
description is an explanation, though
not always the one you're waiting for or know

how to use. Here the joining of rivers
and canals gives rise to so many islands, you
don't notice they're islands, accustomed to
the flowing water and bridges—as though they were
gates to a park, and the number of those who came and of those
who went out again were always the same.

VARIATION ON A THEME FROM DONNE

for B

In Russia I recalled those famous photos,
Earth's greens and blues and whites in a pitch-dark
space Donne could only imagine. We mark
time by change. For Russians: who could go
abroad—visas and passports. For Donne:
where thoughts could travel, *an airy expansion*

of possibilities: distance versus
affection: love as gravity. What draws us,
draws me home. Donne wouldn't have trusted such
apparent special pleading, who argued touch
was less real less than geometry, and the space
we move through, an illusion of emptiness.

TULIPS

Maybe our failed hopes rise like tulips
out of the cold ground,
and, when we look around,
there their satin bowls are, chocolates,

and swaying, velvety clarets, aglow
with memories of help we thought would
appear and beliefs we watered.
And we do have something to show,

goblet-like reminders of our stubborn
labors—or we don't, and refuse
odorless flowers and choose
to live without consolation.

PADUA

Across the bridge, the garbage-swollen stream
that marked the former city wall, we seemed
steered to a small square where Petrarch stood
in bronze, larger than life. Padua could

surprise you like that, and stun you. Past two
a.m., unable to asleep, I padded to
the window, made out the stream, then a swan's
white plumage, gliding down and back again.

What was it doing there? Was I awake?
I still see the taut curve of its neck
caught by the raw brightness of the bridge lights,
aglow, floating in the stillness of the night.

SOMEONE PAUSING

We all need places to leave for and something to leave
behind in them, doors down the hall closing, snatches

of conversation making us stop and look around.
If words were feathery and their spacings, gaps

to be completed by others, windows places
to gather and respond in . . . the clomping of horse-

shoes on cobbles, crack of wind-driven paper, blue
shower of sparks as a tram arm loses contact.

You stand by a busy boulevard at night, the islands
between its lanes, in that muddy city you have loved.

i.

In Venice lapping water masks the hiss
of soft brick and marble crumbling, the slow
decay that even frantic Tintoretto
couldn't extinguish. Mornings, muggy with mist,
dew streaks the mossed slate roofs, and boats pass
with crated endive, eggplants, olives. The smell
of diesel oil spreads, and engine-roars that swell
like a bow-surge or the damped ring of brass,
submerging church, plaza, bridge—and none of these.
The city's less canals than shadows, less
palazzi than the muted blues, the twists
of a shoulder or hip in gentle Veronese—
lagoons of rose, tourists. What persists
if not resistance, however futile that is?

ii.

After the expected surprises, this time feels
like others, when something told me I would not
be coming back. If the water shines as hot
tears might, then the churned fog, a caustic, peels
back the grimed layers of self. Air burns,
condensing even as you move against it,
to abrade and scrape clean. Once you've sensed it,
that you're off balance, you compensate. One learns
to feign indifference and its opposite—
extremes are not quite real. Soon syllables
replace experience: Venice, Padua . . .
and someone starts remembering. We comfort
the past by reconstructing it. Anyone might fill
the glasses, anyone toast who we once were.

STANDOUTS

Nobody went away, not yet—
they're all still here, but very quiet:

the boy famous for wiggling his ears,
the girl who could bend back her fingers—

they just haven't come up with a new thrill
or way of attracting notice. Still,

they could both be teachers now, or, could be
one's into driving trucks, the other, money,

both practicing when it's late? They could,
though I too doubt the likelihood.

But rule out nothing. You pick up the phone
when it rings, say hello, no rhyme or reason

to calls. For a moment the possibilities
impossibly expand, then freeze.

Remember the guy who played bridge like a pro,
and the one with a book out? You never know.

PARAKEET

Mornings, she'd hop on my shoulder for a ride,
take off to the blinds, or like a lover, nibble
my earlobe with such persistence I had to
brush her off—and struggled through illness
as though called back. When I saw her

on her side and righted her, she allowed me
to stroke her flank and head with my finger,
keeping herself upright, vertical, just tipping
forward, stretching her neck out, black eyes
undimmed, without sound or stir, as she died.

Her absence hovers like a swelling drop,
the words she almost knew in two languages.
She'd roll a pencil to the table edge,
watch it stall, then lower her beak and push,
nudging it forward again, and wait for the crash.

BLUE HERON

It stands shin-deep in a shallow run,
blue-gray from back to front,
from side to side, crest-plumes
and black streaks starting at the eye,
compact and composed. Or it assumes
another pose, neck held high
and motionless above the glass-
smooth, metal-bright surface
of the water, waiting to blend in
like trees and stones. The beak, when

it spears a small fish, often
tossing it in the air first,
then opening wide to swallow, can
be frightening. Is this all rehearsed—
the speed, the nonchalance and easy
gulp of the meal, its immobility
only a ruse, a studied act,
or a highly refined survival tactic?
Steal quietly, trip or stumble
down the bank though, and it will

turn toward you, heavily, as it
senses your presence, then with effort,
bend at the knees and push off,
leaping, neck stretched aloft
to assist. It will lift itself airward,
awkward wings extended, rapid
down beats smoothing, each absurd,
bamboo-knobby leg under
it tucked in now like a belly feather
and land flowing below the bird.

THE TROUBLE WITH SPRING

The warmth is welcome, the green seeping into
stems, chickadees drilling the air
with their staccato nonsense. There's no harm
in any of that. Even the gnats, like pepper
on the wall, are only annoying. But the lack of blue

sky, the pall of clouds, that constant lead-
gray above, sloping my shoulders, the weight of time
bending and pulling, oppress me. It's all in your head,
you say, but if so, the shadows inside are still outside
like a burden, and intolerable—no breaking free

of the self, no integrity to subject/
object distinctions. Thank God spring's not stubborn,
even if that requires the same of fall.
I reject sameness, blurred edges. Let other people
and clear skies flourish, worlds beside our own

for escaping to and through: windows, back doors.
Maybe spring's not so bad, and anticipation
is a kind of heightening delay to be pleased
by when it ends abruptly as with a gun
shot—which is not to say I want more.

My mother and her sister, Esther, though they were identical twins, were never the same. My sister lists their differences—from the sorts of men they married, to the one's love of adventure, the other's placidness. Still, when Esther married, a year later my mother did, and within months their apartments and houses were a short walk away. When Esther's husband retired to a condo in Florida, in a year my mother found one that faced it at an angle across the Inland Waterway. They would call each other throughout the day. The evening after my mother's funeral, my cousins, my wife, and my sister were at Esther's having dinner. Alone in the kitchen, Esther, who didn't believe in an afterlife, turned to me: *I always thought we would go together.*

IV

VALENTINE

Say the heart's principal industry is worry
and an irregular pulse doesn't imply
someone mired in debt and bad luck
brought it on himself, though
the lines in your face may have
revealed more than you intended,

and the wrong decisions a son makes,
their awful repetitions, though they
chill your blood, can
no more stop its flow than pain
always peaks or any reassurance
is better than none, empty

cheer. Say we're married to clarity,
that we can't lie to ourselves to
save ourselves. Maybe compassion
doesn't start at home. Maybe
spaces open out, ice-stars glinting
in the tall weeds, without

so much as a hint
of maliciousness and ospreys, bright-sided
rainbow trout . . . and the telephone
poles, lined up
at attention, bring news
as harmless as their ringing.

AMONG THE DEAD

Between the station wagons, the pickups in raw
gray primer and puddles known to easily swallow
a man alive, I spot Owen—his half-lit
smile and that bemused look that spreads
across the faces of twins. I make as though
to wave, then catch myself, recalling he's dead.

It's someone else, of course. Another day,
I'd swear it was Conrad I'd almost collided with, saw
marching down the street at a furious pace,
stick in hand, beheading flowers, although
he collapsed and died in a stairwell months before.
I've read of ghosts. I always thought they glowed

the way headlights in a rearview mirror do.
Who could have guessed they sneaked off, frightened
of each other's company, would adopt our moves,
our bodies when these came available—like fire
using what's there—that we might live among them
as among hopes and inexpressible desires.

STROKES

The first time I found my father on the floor
was in the basement. I was fifteen. He
was coming round. It's nothing, he said, the only
trace of fear he hadn't scoured: sour

breath. Sitting up in a hospital bed,
he told me he'd fallen in the office entrance,
that he found himself places—with nonchalance,
as if at a certain point everyone started

waking fully dressed. And later, gown
tied, but open in the back, a glass
of water at his bedside where his false
teeth had soaked overnight, he was none

too happy to see me, or have me see him unshaved,
unsteady. I was closer to twenty by that time,
and he was embarrassed. Before the strokes killed him,
he'd have to relearn walking, but was saved

a final shame. In that hospital room, his eyes
focus when I take his hand, his lips
move. Then someone he'd mumble to slips
behind this person he doesn't recognize.

ON CERTAINTY

Maybe certainty is growing old
all at once, finding you stand on ice
thick enough to support you. The cold
creaks beneath, or maybe it's only lies.

Think of the sick man, the accident victim
at that moment when he knows
clearly there is no saving him—
his, the certainty you crave. Suppose,

unwittingly, we just go on mixing hope
with understanding, until the horizon
shrinks to a point, or a single note
blots the rest out, and we've nothing to pick from.

Doesn't it fit the endings we intuit—
of innocence, of love—their calm
extent, the almost infinite
flatness they leave us going on and on?

TALONICHKAYA VODKA

—for Maya

At the table where your father once told me "There isn't good vodka or bad vodka; there's only more and less," we talk about Soviet customs with that piquant pleasure only people who have shared the experiences of a vanished world can know. You mention a theatre in Tblisi. People went there, you say, because the food was the best in town. After the curtain went up, a waiter would drift in from the buffet and announce the first row's *khinkali* were ready, and the first row would file out. Then it would be the second row's turn.

In Tallinn, when I first worked in the Soviet Union, pay included the ration coupons needed to buy cigarettes, vodka, soap—so many per month. *Talons*, they were called, or, more affectionately, *talonichki*. I gave the ones for soap to my landlady, and in return she did my laundry, and I traded cigarette talonichki for soap or vodka talons.

Several years after the Soviet Union's demise, I attended a party in St. Petersburg, that name then only recently restored. The long table every one sat around was heavy with pickled mushrooms, radish and beet salads swimming in sour cream, meat or cabbage stuffed rolls; there was good Moldavian white wine and suspect Georgian red, "Soviet" champagne, and a number of different vodkas. Guests kept arriving with contributions.

The feast had already begun when a latecomer opened a paper sack, withdrawing a half-liter of vodka, the old sort that once opened can't be resealed. Everyone grew excited. *"Talonichkaya vodka?"* A nod. The bottle, a survivor of another time, was passed around and everyone filled a little glass. Maybe there was a salute to hardships endured or youth—I don't remember what was toasted, certainly not the good old days. There isn't good nostalgia or bad nostalgia.

ACCIDENT

Are you okay? When I answered *yes*, adding
I'd already called it in and was waiting for
the tow-truck, she blessed me from the cab,
then Jesus for preserving me, then got down.
You've no idea when the tow truck will show up;
you might stand in the cold for hours, she said,
moving beside the truck, which, like her,
had been around, rummaging in her sacks
of groceries and pulled a bagel out. *No*
thanks, I said. She insisted. It was easier
to accept than fight with her, and besides,
there was something so natural, so direct,
for all the bless Jesus-es, the bagel, so
soft, topped with burnt onions, garlic chips,
so bereft of any *yiddishkeit* . . . I took it,
like her benediction, with a nod, a Jew,
ankle-deep in snow on a rural road in
eastern Washington, car down the steep
embankment, cradled by cattails. How
had I come to be there, hand around a roll
as much a bagel as I was a Jew, I wondered?
Only a deity who delighted in far-fetched
scenarios could have concocted a delivery
like that. Before I took a bite, rather than
a *motsi*, I peered at my precariously balanced
car, then into the shimmering distance
from whence the wrecker would come.
Hat on, I blessed her and my good fortune.

EMPTY PLACES

Mother was gone when I arrived,
as if we'd passed and she was alive,
though somewhere else. I brooded through
the funeral, then left—her view,

her mono-climate, cards, the books
I'd sent, stopping for one last look.
And stored it all away like the house
of my childhood, where a city bus

geared down at the corner, and overhead
planes began their noisy descent
on LaGuardia's glidepath. They'd rock
our floors and walls. The talk would stop

like halted movie frames, then leap,
reanimated, not a beat
dropped, though slivers we hardly missed
escaped as sighs, laments or hisses.

ORDERS

1.

Among the young, uniformed food-servers
along the glassed-in counter behind which
trays of sliced cold cuts and cheeses gleam
there's an order—who's deferential to
whom, who moves, who doesn't, shoulder feints, side-
steps, shrunken, abbreviated to save
the busy energy and time—nothing
you'd notice, though they know each of them cold.

2.

A paper littered table. The bosses
chat, straighten their ties, one, jacketed,
sitting, another, shirt sleeves rolled, darting
off to snatch a tray left uncleared, napkins
from the floor, as if there were hierarchies here
too. Of the two guys sweeping, which one is
moving up? You guess. You make assumptions:
how long do you think you can sit before
you're told, *Seats are for paying customers*?

3.

Did you know Tokyo restaurants closed
for the Olympic Games? They had no way
to gauge the social rank of foreigners,
which Japanese grammar requires for
polite address. Once rent, the whole social
fabric just might unravel at your feet.

4.

Light and open, the atrium roof
five floors up—don't you feel protected from
the elements? Or do the stray people
sauntering by and those at work seem to
say, *Nowhere is safe*. If no one comes up
to tap you on the shoulder, does that mean
everyone knows the rules and plays by them,
or does fear, *what if,* bark out the orders?

LINES

There are no straight lines in nature.

The edge between lit and shadowed
foliage in the grove is straight enough
to lay a course by, though it points

nowhere. The tree trunks, not quite
half round, set it humming a semi-
quaver, adding their minor ripples

like overtones. And winds shaking
the leaves, which are the insubstantial
body of the trees at any distance, blur

a keener division. There's the sharp
horizon, like a bow at rest, curved so
gradually it can run on for mile after

slow mile before you catch on—cracks
in ice, in rock faces, slip-planes, faults
where the earth heaves and breathes.

LIGHTNESS

Isn't reading like sleep, another place
to leave yourself? The way air bears you—it's
as if you'd thrown the blankets back for a taste
of bracing cold. Put the book down,
your secret life, each sober calculation.
The wind's alive. Air's erasing the horizon.

MARK HALPERIN

taught at Central Washington University and has taught
in Japan, Estonia, Russia, and Ukraine. His poetry books
have been published by the University of Pittsburgh
Press, Wesleyan University Press, and Copper Canyon Press.
His poems and translations have appeared in a variety of
journals. Halperin lives outside of Ellensburg, Washington,
near the Yakima River.